When the Monkeys Came Back

Other Books by Kristine L. Franklin

The Old, Old Man and the Very Little Boy
The Shepherd Boy

Also Illustrated by Robert Roth

And in the Beginning...
(by Sheron Williams)

When the Monkeys Came Back

Kristine L. Franklin

Illustrated by

Robert Roth

ATHENEUM 1994 NEW YORK
Maxwell Macmillan Canada
Toronto
Maxwell Macmillan International
New York Oxford Singapore Sydney

Atheneum
Macmillan Publishing Company
866 Third Avenue
New York, NY 10022

Maxwell Macmillan Canada, Inc.
1200 Eglinton Avenue East
Suite 200
Don Mills, Ontario M3C 3N1

Macmillan Publishing Company is part of the
Maxwell Communication Group of Companies.

First edition
Printed in Singapore on recycled paper
10 9 8 7 6 5 4 3 2 1
The text of this book is set in Quorum Book.
The illustrations are rendered in watercolors.

Library of Congress Cataloging-in-Publication Data

Franklin, Kristine L.
When the monkeys came back / by Kristine L. Franklin; illustrated by Robert Roth. —1st ed.
p. cm.
Summary: Always remembering how the monkeys in her Costa Rican valley disappeared when all the trees were cut down, Marta grows up, plants more trees, and sees the monkeys come back.
ISBN 0-689-31807-3
[1. Monkeys—Fiction. 2. Costa Rica—Fiction. 3. Trees—Fiction.
4. Conservation of natural resources—Fiction.] I. Roth, Robert, ill.
II. Title.
PZ7.F859226Wh 1994
[E]—dc20 92-33684

To my children, Kelly and Jody,
who heard the monkeys with me
K. L. F.

To my little girl, Cassidy
R. R.

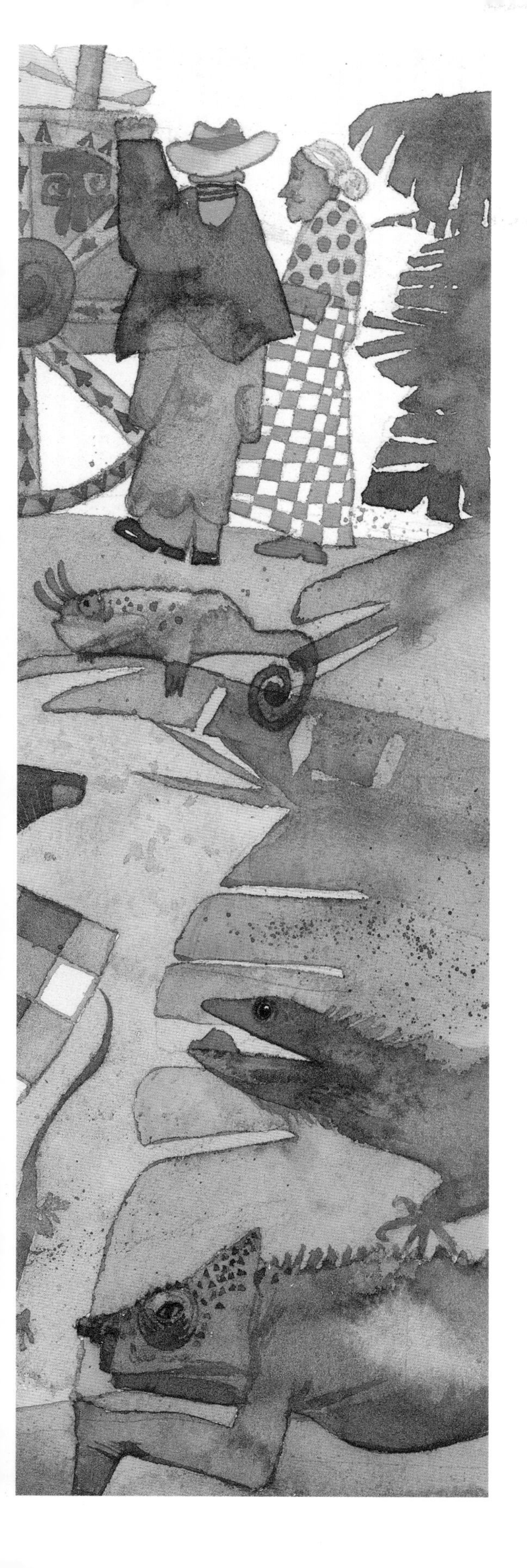

When Doña Marta was a very little girl, the valley was a peaceful place. Children giggled as they chased each other between rows of tall corn. Fathers whistled as they dug in the gardens. Mothers hummed softly as they wrapped black beans and cornmeal in banana leaves to cook.

There was one old road in the valley, but it was an ox-cart road, an open place for meeting friends or cousins, a nice place for walking, a sunny place for catching lizards. There weren't any cars at all. The valley was a quiet place, except when the monkeys called.

Every morning and every evening for as long as anyone could remember, the monkeys announced the changing of night into day, the changing of day into night. At dawn they would howl and bark to one another, and the noise they made was like thunder in the trees. At dusk they would hoot and scream, and each leaf and each blade of grass would tremble from the sound.

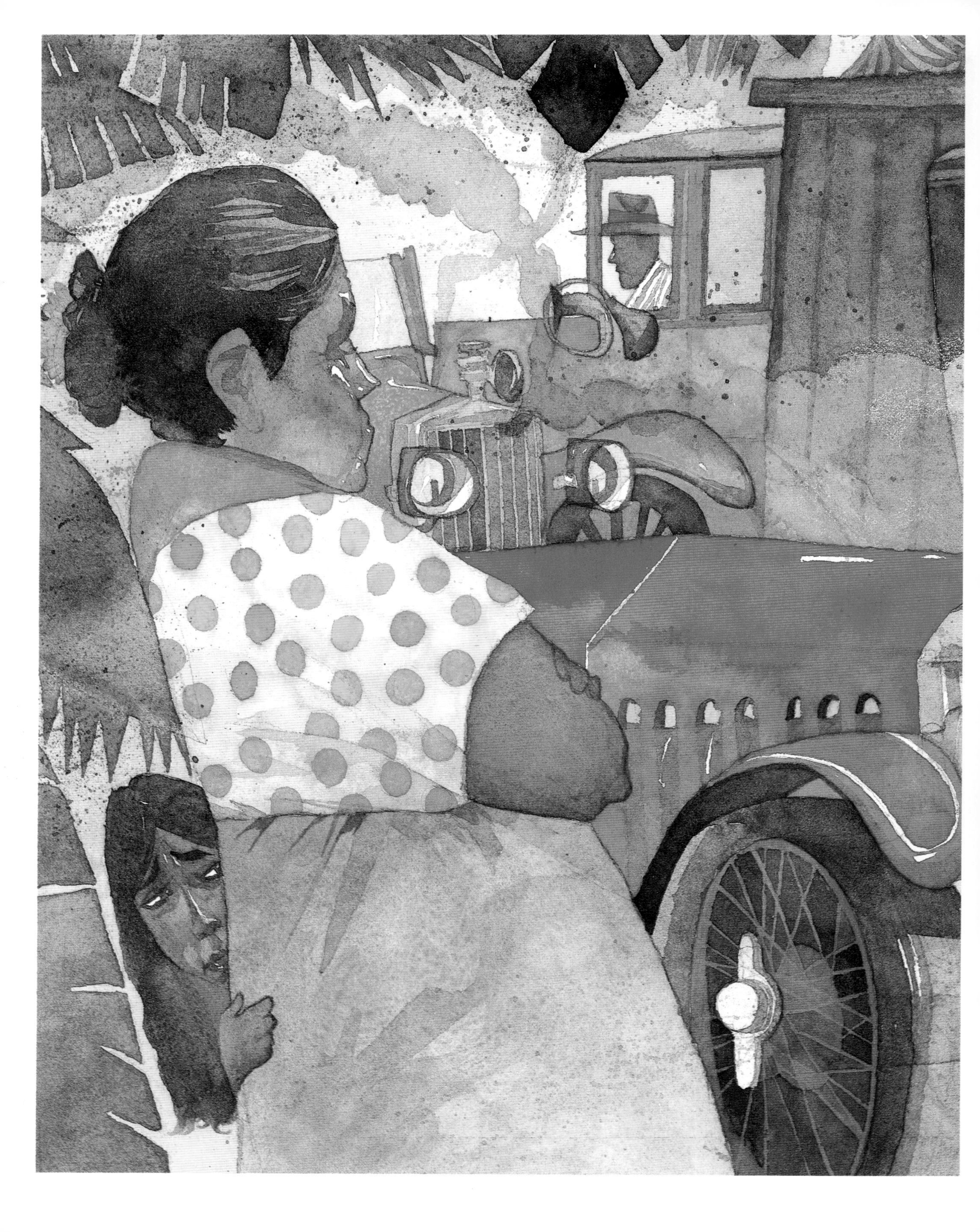

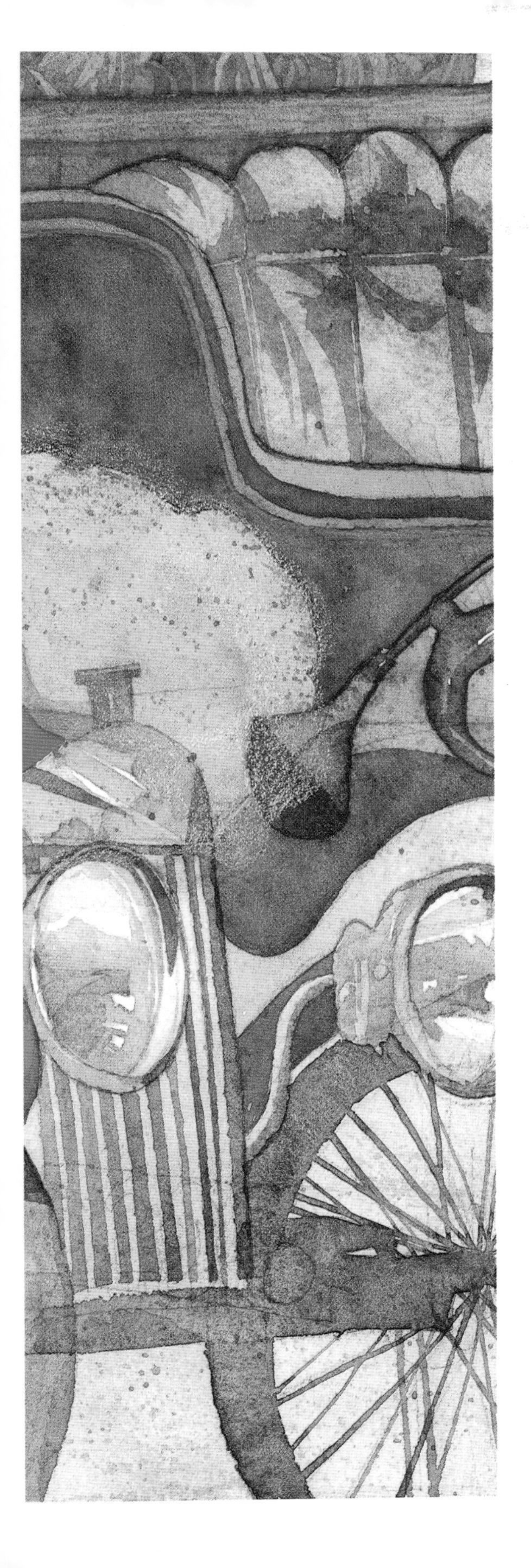

One day a car chugged and spluttered up the old road. After that more cars came, not many at first, for the road was an ox road, not a car road. Marta was afraid of the cars. The sound and smell made her hide behind her mother's skirt. More and more cars came, and trucks, and more noise. Before long it wasn't safe to walk down the middle of the road, to stand and talk, to chase the quick lizards.

Still the monkeys shouted from the trees, drowning out all the new noises for a few moments each day, hooting to one another as they always had, waking up the world in the morning, calling the workers home from the fields at night.

The rains came and went and Marta's dress grew too short, and one day some men from the city came to Marta's house. They offered her father a lot of money, enough to buy six cows *and* a brand new dress for Marta, and asked to cut down some trees on the side of the mountain. Marta's father agreed and from that day on, the forest began to disappear.

At first it was just a few trees. The lumbermen cut down only the biggest trees, the ones with the hanging vines. The monkeys didn't seem to mind. They howled and barked and scolded just as before. But five years later, when there were only twenty-four trees left in the forest, the monkeys went away.

Marta didn't know where the monkeys went. One night, just as the sun slipped behind the hills, the monkeys shrieked and hooted and cried, louder than ever before. Some said it was because of the full moon. Others said the rainy season was near. But the next morning the valley was as silent as a stone.

Over the next several years the last of the trees was cut down. What had once been a forest was now covered with stumps and tangled brush. There were a few birds but no monkeys.

Most people forgot about the monkeys. They had roosters to wake them up in the morning, lamps to work by at night. But Marta didn't forget.

When she was fifteen years old Marta married Emilio. Emilio worked for Marta's father and when her father died, he left his farm to Marta and Emilio.

"You have a lot of land now," said Marta one day. "I would like to have some of it for myself." Emilio laughed out loud, because in those days, women did not own land.

"Soon we will have a family to feed," said Emilio. "After I plant corn and beans and squash, there will be nothing left over to give you. The rest of the land belongs to the cows."

"What about the land on the side of the mountain?" asked Marta. "There are too many stumps for a garden. And it is too steep for cows."

"That's true," agreed Emilio, and though it went against the custom, he gave the land on the side of the mountain to Marta.

"What are you going to do with your land?" asked Emilio.

"I'm going to bring back the forest," said Marta, and that is what she did.

Marta planted trees from the foot of the mountain to as far up as she could climb. When the sun baked the ground in the dry season, she hauled buckets of water to the trees. When the hard rains washed the little trees from the soil, she gently replanted them.

Year after year, Marta took care of the trees. In the next fifteen years she gave birth to eleven children. Each child learned to plant and tend trees. Year after year, Marta's children grew tall and so did the trees.

"Coffee grows well on a mountain," Emilio would tease. "Maybe you could plant coffee on your land." But Marta didn't listen. She didn't change her mind, and the forest came back.

SAN

Many more years passed. The trees grew higher and higher. Marta's children grew up and had children of their own. Emilio died and left the farm to Marta and her sons.

One day old Doña Marta took a walk along the road in the warm sunshine. The children greeted her as she passed.

"Good morning, Tree Lady," they said.

"Good morning," answered Doña Marta with a wink and an old, old smile. She leaned on her stick and stared across the valley.

Her trees touched the sky. Thick vines wrapped around their trunks. Birds of every color filled their branches. Now, wherever they dropped their seeds, new trees would grow. The valley was bright with squash and corn and beans, but the side of the mountain was a deep, dark green, forest green. Doña Marta's work was finished.

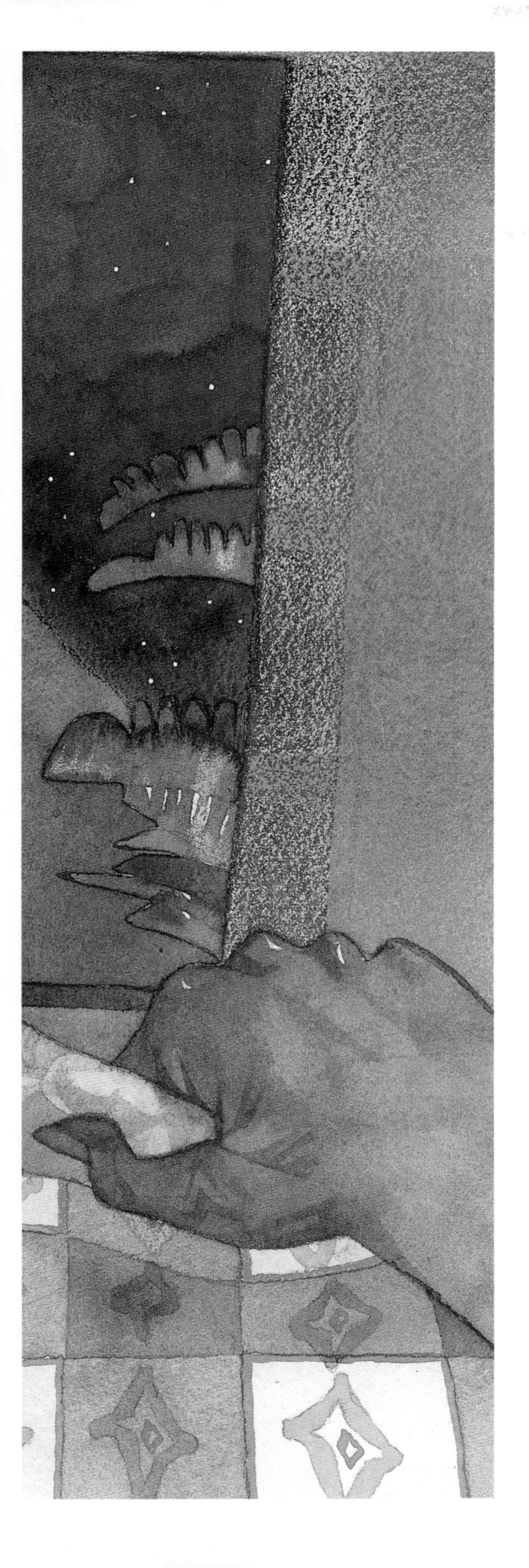

One night, Doña Marta couldn't sleep. As she lay in her bed she listened to the sounds of insects, the twittering of the night birds. Out her little window she watched the stars trail across the black sky. She watched the moon shadows shift and change in her room. As dawn approached, she heard the roosters begin to crow. And then she heard another sound.

At first it sounded like the barking of dogs, but soon the barking turned into howling, the howling into shrieks, the shrieks into shouts, and every leaf and every blade of grass trembled with the sound. Doña Marta hobbled to the window and leaned out.

The dark air thundered with the sound of monkeys hooting, howling, screaming from the treetops, waking up the whole world once again. Doña Marta closed her eyes, smiled a wrinkled smile, and listened to the music she had missed for fifty-six long years.

Every morning now, old Doña Marta wakes up to the barking and scolding of the monkeys. Every evening she waits for them to gather in the trees to shriek and howl and say good night. For a few moments each morning and evening, the sound of the monkeys drowns out all the other sounds in the valley. For a few moments each day, it's as if nothing had ever changed.